Bright Sparks

The Elves and the Shoemaker

p

Helping your child read

Bright Sparks readers are closely linked to recognized learning strategies. Their vocabulary has been carefully selected from word lists recommended by educational experts.

Read the story

Read the story
to your child
a few times.

When it was time for bed, the
shoemaker hid.
Soon the two elves came out to play.
They saw the leather.
They saw the shoes and boots cut out.
The elves sewed the shoes.
Then they sewed the boots.
They sewed them very neatly.
"What kind elves," the shoemaker said
to himself.

Follow your finger

Run your finger under
the text as you read.
Soon your child will begin to
follow the words with you.

Look at the pictures

Talk about the pictures. They will
help your child understand the story.

The shoemaker hid.

21

Give it a try

Let your child try
reading the large
type on each
right-hand page.
It repeats a line
from the story.

Join in

When your child is ready,
encourage him or her to join in with
the main story text. Shared reading
is the first step to reading alone.

Once a shoemaker and his wife
lived in a shoe shop.
They were very poor.
One day, the shoemaker had only
one piece of leather left.
It was very small.
The shoemaker cut out some shoes and
went to bed.

The shoemaker cut out
some shoes.

That night, two elves came out to play.
They saw the leather.
They saw the shoes cut out.
So the elves sewed the shoes.
They sewed them very neatly.

The elves sewed the shoes.

The next morning, the shoemaker
found the shoes.
"What lovely shoes!" he said.
Just then, a woman came into the
shoe shop.
She tried on the shoes.
"These shoes are just right," she said.
She gave the shoemaker some money.

"These shoes are just right."

The shoemaker bought a big
piece of leather.
He cut out some boots and went
to bed.
That night, the two elves came out to
play again.
They saw the leather.
They saw the boots cut out.
So the elves sewed the boots.
They sewed them very neatly.

The elves sewed the boots.

The next morning the shoemaker found
the boots.
"What lovely boots!" he said.
Just then, a man came into the
shoe shop.
He took off his shoes and tried on the
boots.
"These boots are just right," he said.
He gave the shoemaker some money.

"These boots are just right."

The shoemaker bought a bigger piece
of leather.

He cut out some shoes and some boots.

"Who is making the shoes and boots?"
said the shoemaker's wife.

"I will find out!" said the shoemaker.

"I will hide and see who comes to make
them for me."

"Who is making the shoes
and boots?"

When it was time for bed, the
shoemaker hid.
Soon the two elves came out to play.
They saw the leather.
They saw the shoes and boots cut out.
The elves sewed the shoes.
Then they sewed the boots.
They sewed them very neatly.
"What kind elves," the shoemaker said
to himself.

The shoemaker hid.

The shoemaker told his wife about
the elves.
"How can we thank them?" he said.
"Let's make shoes for them!" said the
shoemaker's wife.
The shoemaker got his finest piece of
leather.
Then they made some tiny shoes.

They made some tiny shoes.

Then the shoemaker and his wife hid.
Soon the elves came out to play.
They tried on the tiny shoes.
The tiny shoes were perfect.

The tiny shoes were perfect.

After that, lots of people came to buy the shoes and boots at the shoe shop. And the shoemaker and his wife were never poor again.

They were never poor again.

Look back in your book.
Can you read these words?

shoemaker

shoes

wife

elves

boots

shoe shop

Can you answer these questions?

Who bought some shoes?

Who bought some boots?

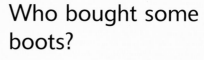

Who made the shoes for the shoemaker?

The End